# PICNIC GROUNDS

## *a* NOVEL IN FRAGMENTS

BY OZ SHELACH

Cover image: detail of *Partition Line*
(oil on canvas, 2002) by David Goss
Flyleaves: detail of *100 Gr.*
(oil on wood parquet, 1999) by David Goss

Cover design by Yolanda Montijo
Book design by Elaine Katzenberger
Typography by Harvest Graphics

Library of Congress Cataloging-in-Publication Data

Shelach, Oz, 1968-
Picnic grounds : a novel in fragments / by Oz Shelach.
p. cm.
ISBN 0-87286-419-7
Israel—Fiction. I. Title.

PR9510.9.S53 P5 2003
823'.92—dc21 2002041270

Oz Shelach would like to hug Ammiel Alcalay, Vijay Seshadri, Elaine Katzenberger, and Yael Lerer.

Visit our web site: www.citylights.com

CITY LIGHTS BOOKS are edited by Lawrence Ferlinghetti and Nancy J. Peters and published at the City Lights Bookstore, 261 Columbus Avenue, San Francisco, CA 94133

For my sisters
Samera and Tzlil

# PICNIC GROUNDS

## *a* NOVEL IN FRAGMENTS

## ONE AFTERNOON

A PROFESSOR OF HISTORY FROM BAYIT VA-GAN TOOK his family for a picnic in a quiet pinewood near Giv'at Shaul, formerly known as Deir Yassin. It was not too cold to be in the shade and not too warm to build a fire, so the professor passed on to his son camping skills he had acquired in the army. They arranged three square stones in a U, to block the wind, leaving access on the fourth side. They stacked broken branches on top of twigs on top of dry pine needles. He let his son put a match to it. Listening carefully, they heard a faint low hum from the curves of the winding highway, hidden from view by the trees. The professor did not talk of the village, origin of the stones. He did not talk of the village school, now a psychiatric hospital, on the other side of the hill. He imagined that he and his family were having a picnic, unrelated to the village; enjoying its grounds outside history.

which bore the same name, Sa'Sa'; then stealing across the border to Egypt. We came to stay several days on the beach that—we remembered, longing for our lost naiveté—we had once called *ours*, and which remained unsullied by development. The waiter's tranquility, on a characteristically mellow beach in Sinai, made him all the more attractive to us. We wanted him to address us by our first names, we wanted to give him a generous tip, even a pair of good sandals, but because of the openness with which he told us his story we could see no point in trying to assuage him. He had inhabited 'Ayn Al-Helweh camp at the exact same period when the child, on whom the great Palestinian cartoon character was to be based, inhabited it. He told us how he had assisted a young boy away from a massacre, arranged a makeshift bed for him, and lullabied him to sleep. The boy was barefoot when he found him, and bald but for a dozen short bristles. He lay face down, blood trickling from his ankle, his hands crossed behind his back. For months, our waiter carried Hanthalah every morning from his own wet tent, into the dry tent of the clinic, and in a nearby village had a seamstress patch the boy's shirt elbow. He was the first to see the boy dead. At that time, he could not have known who Hanthalah, over whose dead face he drew the blanket, was to become.

## THE HOUSE

GHOSTS DON'T SAY MUCH, OUR FRIEND TOLD US whose only daughter and husband were killed in two bomb attacks, one in a pedestrian shopping district in West Jerusalem and the other on the street next to a bus-bomb. Standing in line for the buffet at our mutual friends' party, she said that ghosts' best, richest performance is in dreams, but those visits have become rare in her life as she masturbates more frequently. One evening, after a whole week shut in at home and crying, she knelt on the living room floor, called out to her daughter, and saw her sitting on the couch, hands in her lap. She wanted to touch her daughter's shoulder. Twelve years older, there was no mistaking her smile. "It's all right," her daughter said, "you could not have saved me." But our friend remembered how she had wished her daughter dead, had known she would make good use of the estate and enjoy having the family house all to herself.

# TEL-AVIVIANS IN JERUSALEM

All Jerusalemites are familiar with the anxious, lost look on the face of strangers—peeking out of their car windows, usually a couple, or a larger group—and their question, "How do we get out?" They long for the safety of their own merry city, where, as if in a bubble, they think they can forget where they really are, where the orthodox Jews know their place, and the Arabs obediently wash dishes in restaurants. We, who know our way through all the narrow alleys, as well as the wider winding streets and the recently bulldozed express-roads that cut through the mountainous slopes of our city at impossibly straight angles, know also that this sense of being trapped in a maze is the foundation, the very essence even, of Jerusalem. Therefore we direct the Tel-Avivians deeper in, closer to the heart of the city.

# A TRAITOR

In Tel-Aviv, at the opening session of the Botanical Society's annual meeting, a presentation by a botanist from Haifa was cancelled at the last minute, and replaced by a panel on ethics before which the said botanist was to testify. That year his explorations had taken him to an anemone field near Bayt-Shemesh, which confirmed what he had read in the history books but never had seen for himself: long strips of white, blue, and purple anemones ran through the thick of the red ones, like veins. His crime lay in publishing the site of his finding in an independent magazine. After questioning by the prominent members of the panel, he was condemned as a traitor, and a motion to expel him from the Botanical Society was accepted unanimously. The researcher tried to defend himself by claiming he had faithfully documented, as was his job, on film and in measurements, the various shades of anemones in the Yehuda plain, but his colleagues could not forgive him.

## REPLACEMENT

THE OLDEST, MOST EXPERIENCED WAITER IN JERUSALEM worked, appropriately, in the oldest and most respectable bar, established by one of the R's early in the 1920s to serve him and his guests when he visited the country. It was, in our opinion, and still is, the only bar in the city that deserves to be called a bar. Lawyers and accountants frequent it, businessmen, journalists, politicians, and artists whose works—exchanged for alcohol—decorate the walls. We loved to watch the waiter's graceful walk among the tables in the small, dark, red-draped room, and frequently remarked that his talent to foresee patrons' wishes even before these were expressed made him an establishment in his own right. When we ran out of conversation we bet the next round on the next unannounced race between the waiter and the proprietor to reach—lighter in hand—a patron's cigarette. We thought: this waiter knows the truth about all of us, and unlike the proprietor, keeps his mouth shut. One afternoon the waiter did not show up for work and could not be traced. Among ourselves we complained about his replacement, a fawning man with a bow tie and a heavy Eastern European accent, but soon *he* became known as the oldest, most experienced waiter in Jerusalem.

## WAKING UP

A GUEST AT A WEDDING WE WERE INVITED TO, IN THE Jerusalem Forest—a picnic with few servants and simple dresses—imagined the trees were swarming with highwaymen and ferocious animals. "Robbers!" he cried out when he thought he could discern movement among the pines, "Wolves! Beasts!" We attributed this poor comedy—by a man we all knew for a certified drunkard, who knew as well as we all did that the whole wood we call the Jerusalem Forest lies only five minutes away from the surrounding neighborhoods and is nothing more than a buffer strip between luxury residential areas and the highway to Tel-Aviv—to this guest's upbringing in communist Russia. The drunkard got hold of a bottle of special liqueur, privately imported from the Czech Republic and brought to the wedding by another guest, and wandered off into the trees. When asked, some days later, about his disappearance, he said the drink was bitter and more potent than anything that ever went down his throat, and that his last recollection of himself was sitting on the asphalt of an unknown street, waving his hands over his head, having lost his eyesight. However, after two days, he woke up in his room, which was much cleaner than he could ever remember, and found two containers of fat-free yogurt in the refrigerator. He could see.

## AN EXAMPLE

My first assignment as a conscript reporter for the army radio station was to cover the trial of an old man accused of Nazi war crimes, from the preliminary hearings to the trial's inevitable culmination in a death sentence. The Ministry of Trials rented a movie theater and promptly converted it into a courthouse for the trial, at the gates to which the audience, bussed in from all over the country, formed long lines. Every day, from eight-thirty in the morning to one o'clock in the afternoon, and from four in the afternoon to seven at night, court sessions were broadcast live to our numerous listeners. My job was to fill in lulls in litigation, to tell the listeners whose voice they were hearing, to interview high-ranking officers from the army, politicians, famous survivors and other celebrities who attended the trial sessions, and to summarize the proceedings at the end of each session. When at last the judges read out their sentence there was a commotion in the audience and an outburst of singing: *'Am Yisrael Hai*, "The People of Israel Live." Some years later, the high court reversed the verdict, ruling that the accused had been misidentified, could not, in fact, have been the war criminal of whose crimes he was convicted, and pronounced him not guilty. We all agreed it was a shining example of our honest System of Trials. The three judges who had signed the death sentence were promoted, naturally, to the high court.

# HELP

ON THE FLIGHT FROM BANGKOK TO DELHI WE SAT next to a woman whose parents, a year after her only brother's death in a car accident, went on vacation to France and left her alone. Grieving, she swallowed some pills and slept for a whole day, waking up with a piercing stomachache. A week later, when her parents came back, she did not tell them, and they were so insensitive as to remind her that Friday had been her brother's birthday, on which they had chosen to be away. Since that time, the woman told us and a nurse who was sitting in the next row, she makes sure to be away from Israel on her brother's birthday, as well as on her parents' birthdays, on her own birthday, and during major holidays. We tried to help by inviting her to dinner, to mark her brother's birthday and perhaps tell us more about him. But she said, with a crumpled face, that she would rather not come, that she hates being reminded of that date. She then moved to another seat, away from us.

## BEING FIRST

In the fourth grade of Bayt HaKerem primary school, we took a class trip to see unusual pines: darker than in most picnic grounds, taller, with longer pairs of needles. We knelt and brushed aside the thick carpet of dry brown needles with our hands. Pine nuts lay on the exposed ground. When we had a bagful we laid them one by one on a flat rock and broke the hard shells with another rock; we landed on them from above, crash, we broke the brown-black-stained shell and out came small soft nuts, soft ivory fat small nuts. It was late in the season, but no one had collected before us.

# REGRET

A CRÊPE KIOSK OPERATOR WHO WENT TO HIGH school with us, and whom we remembered as a cheerful youth (he liked to play with the kids in the kindergarten next door) and a troublemaker, told us he was planning to take training offered by the Ministry of Labor and become a chef. We were surprised to see his face peeping out of the street booth, and on realizing how anxious he was for someone to talk to we decided to stop and chat with him, which we had not done for many years. He promised us his crêpes were reliably crisp, the way, he said, crêpes should be, and also recommended the soup, in which he was openly and emotionally invested. Although it was a sad failure, we said the soup was very good, then said it was very good again, then said, more to ourselves than to our high school friend, who seemed to be ignoring us, that clearly there was no one to converse with in this booth. When finally he raised his eyes from the cutting board behind the glass counter, he said that yes, he was there, he had heard it all, he was just highly focused. Sometimes he can not respond, he said, but he hears very well all the same, you simply need to learn to know him, he told us, to understand. We had heard that he could not recover from death squad service. "It isn't those who deserved it," he then told me, "it's those that did not deserve it that I regret." After the army, he joined a special riot-dispersal unit of the police, expecting to feel at home, but was soon discharged for disciplinary problems. Our lawyer friend, with whom he had been a troublemaker at school, the very friend with whom, while on leave from the army, he had once turned a small forest into an improvised shooting gallery, then, into ashes, by mistakenly shooting tracers, told him he ought to sue the Ministry of Security for his inability to adapt to a job.

## AN ORIGINAL

A PROFESSOR OF PHILOSOPHY INHABITED A LARGE OLD house in Baqa'a, which had all the usual properties of large old houses in Jerusalem: stone walls, arched ceilings, an original, still-bearing walnut tree, an original underground cistern, and a well on which the garden was maintained in dry years. His reputation as a broad thinker was amplified by a proven ability to out-argue his colleagues in their own fields. For a while children were allowed to play in the garden, but in the summer of 1967 the professor followed the example of the famous millionaire S and ordered a tall stone wall to be constructed around the house and garden, to prevent the original inhabitants of the house from visiting.

## VACUUM

AT THE TEL-AVIV AIRPORT, WAITING FOR A FLIGHT OUT, we noticed a poet from Tel-Aviv, buying cartons of menthol cigarettes and cheap local brandy. In his youth, early on in the colonization, the poet had been associated with a pioneer militia, which prided itself on its violent attacks on the British, as well as its ruthless struggle against the locals. When asked by his friends in the militia to translate a manual for an English gun, the poet found a vocabulary vacuum on weapons in Hebrew—a language that preceded guns, if not violence—and had to invent words for trigger, bolt, range, and the like. His talent in these inventions—now household words in the army, the press, and the judicial system—is evident to this day. *Kavenet*, literally *sights*, the name he gave his daughter, is today a popular name for girls in Israel. The poet is mostly remembered for his poem "Sword." We asked him, Are you that poet? He said, No.

## TU B'SHVAT

EACH SPRING, SOMETIMES AS EARLY AS EARLY JANUARY, when almond trees blossom white and pink, the birthday of trees is celebrated throughout Israel. Thousands of boys and girls in white shirts, and foreign donors congregate at designated sites to plant new starts and expand the forest. One boy in our class, however, called the ceremonies fascist and murderous. He said that pines grow acrid needles and shed them, thereby annihilating all other growth, wild flowers, shrubs, and smaller indigenous trees. He said, obviously repeating words he heard at home, that forestation of land that was not formerly forested, but which seems every year to hold fewer marks of stone terraces, as rubble and orchards disappear among and under the pines, is a part of what he called "the big lie of our existence." We had been friends with that boy, but on that celebration of *Tu B'Shvat* did not share with him the customary foods of the holiday, dried figs, dates, and nuts, neatly packed for us by our parents.

# CLAUSE 21

Our lawyer friend, whom we had known since attending the same small kindergarten in Rehavia, and who takes care of our properties, told us about a curious case he had worked on. His client, a mutual friend whose name he disclosed without a smile, had asked him for help in obtaining a final release from active reserve service—thirty or forty night-shifts every year, spent sitting in front of a big screen at the air-force intelligence underground headquarters in the heart of Tel-Aviv—a duty that devastated his already unstable sleep cycle. Our lawyer friend suggested the common path for relief from *miluim*, a visit to a mental health officer. The client, however, wished to avoid the mental clause, commonly known as Clause 21. He asked the lawyer to inquire with the authorities whether conversion to Islam would suffice. At the end of a long correspondence the army confirmed that a reserve soldier who converted to Islam would indeed be dismissed from active reserve duty service. Our friend's release document, however, indicated that he was discharged under the mental clause.

## GUINNESS

IT HAPPENED THAT MOST OF US HAD NOT MADE IT TO the bar by the time the shooting began, but our friend told us that after the first shots were heard everyone who was sitting outside on the sidewalk rushed in—some, although not, of course, himself, forgetting to take their drinks in with them. Then the big window doors were locked, the dark curtains drawn, and the radio turned on, to supplement the sounds that came from the street with official reports from the army and the police. The so-called *Arms of Security* took just a few minutes to gun down the attackers but kept combing the neighborhood for suspects for several hours more, during which residents and inhabitants were ordered to stay indoors. At the moment the doors to the bar were locked, our friend said, the barman announced that all drinks were on the house. Everyone was eager for intoxication, and our friend showed particular urbanity by making what he felt was an homage to Belfast.

"I ordered a Guinness," he sealed his story, emitting a rattling laughter, then said it again and laughed again, and again, with the assumed authority of an informed alcoholic who knows his business.

## A REFLECTION

"PREPOSITIONS DIFFER FROM ONE LANGUAGE TO another in apparent arbitrariness, but they illustrate the presuppositions of a language. . ." Each Tuesday afternoon throughout the fall semester the student was lulled to sleep by her professor's lectures on epistemology. Five of the walls that formed the octagonal classroom were so small that the classroom looked more triangular than octagonal. The door was painted orange in agreement with all the doors of the same octagonal foyer, distinguishing it from the next octagonal foyer, which was governed by lilac, from the next, governed by pale green, and so on until foyer number eight, designed, the student thought, like the entire Hebrew University, to block any view of the outside, to narrow the mind, to keep everyone focused on their own reflections and ignorant of anything important. When she woke up and saw, in the single window, a shining object sticking up into the sky, no other student, nor their professor, was looking out the window. She could not tell it was the setting sun reflected by a minaret-top golden crescent, on the next mountain peak to the east. The sound of shots drifted into the classroom through the window. Beyond the narrow view, in the fold of the valley, our soldiers were mowing down protesters. Then the shiny crescent disappeared into the long shadow cast by the university tower.

# INFECTED

A MEDIOCRE JOURNALIST FROM JERUSALEM, WHOSE true, deepest motivation for writing was getting women into bed, stopped writing in Hebrew, which he claimed is an immoral language constructed to serve imperialist powers and promote murder. Since all other languages available to that writer were, he maintained, just as badly infected, or worse, he stopped writing altogether, and indulged in the killing of time, known in Hebrew as *burning* time.

# DIVERSITY

THE NEW NATURALIST IS DIFFERENT FROM THE TURN-of-the-century naturalist, who personally hunted the last bear in the region and is with us only in memory, as well as in the pages of his autobiography, *The Memoirs of a Hebrew Zoologist.* His contemporary heir, however, continues to pursue a prolific career of research and writing. At a slide-show and lecture held for the general public at A Different Trip Gallery in Tel-Aviv, in response to a question from the audience, the naturalist said there is no indication that fireflies have become extinct. He granted that firefly populations were not tracked, monitored, or studied by any researcher, and that their natural habitat had become extinct, but he insisted there was no indication, or any reason to speculate, that their numbers had dropped, since they are known for their resilience, and probably thrive on the relative abundance of lawns in private gardens, and in parks. From his home in Jerusalem, in Yefe Noff neighborhood, he sends us well-formatted texts full of anecdotes: "This beetle, *Coleopetra Avramina*, I named after my friend Avraham, who fell on duty as an officer in battles over Jerusalem. . . The only specimen ever observed of this spider, *Araneus Mironius*, was found on the slopes of Mount Miron; it has been sitting in a big glass jar on my desk, and not much else is known about it." This naturalist's work, in sharp contradiction to bird-watchers' dry physical descriptions and measurements, is accessible, and readers of all ages love it. The guidebooks he writes, and which we publish, help our readers appreciate the diversity of our homeland's great outdoors.

## ANOTHER VIEW

A SENIOR SURGEON WHO WORKED IN SEVERAL HOSPITALS in Israel acquired, in the course of his long and distinguished medical career, four houses, in the vicinity of the hospitals he worked in. In each house he kept a large garden and a large dog. All four houses were built on terraced mountain slopes and offered the most spectacular views in the country: the pine forested mountains of Jerusalem, sunrise over the lake (in the Galilee), an old oak wood in the Carmel mountain range, and another view.

## THE SUICIDE RULE

A SENIOR EDITOR WHO INSTRUCTED US IN THE CRAFT of news production taught us a rule, which he called the suicide rule, and according to which suicides are not to be reported, for fear that public attention will arouse yet more suicides, a wave of suicides even, which constantly threatens to erupt. No record of suicides is maintained by the state, except for public figures, whose suicides the press alludes to in code, or with the euphemism *Put his hand to his soul*; there is no direct reference to suicide, just as some diseases remain nevernamed in our newspaper—cancer, AIDS, other diseases, always referred to as *a long disease*, *an incurable disease*, or simply *a disease*. By the age of twenty-five, every Israeli is personally acquainted with at least two such unreported deaths.

## CHILDREN OF THE WORLD

At the Israel Museum we visited an exhibition of children's drawings and paintings from all over the world. The children had been asked to depict Jerusalem, and we were amused by the naïve images they produced in gouache, water colors, and colored pencils; images of camels, farmers in tunics and blacks in straw skirts, images that were biblical, and agricultural, and pastoral, African even, so much so that they had no connection to anything we ever painted, and that—we knew from our experience—is the real Jerusalem, where we lived and went to school, and from school to the said exhibition at the Israel Museum.

## ASHES TO ASHES

TWO LOVERS FROM JERUSALEM DROVE WEST ON AN afternoon, to the Arthur Rubinstein memorial, at the edge of a forested mountain. A big orange sun silhouetted the lower hills. On the lime rock path from the small parking lot to the memorial they saw a rabbit's shadow swift among the rocks, found a porcupine's quill among the low shrubs, saw a cave chiseled out of the mountain by the very same goatherds who had had to leave before immigrants were installed nearby in cooperative farms. The two lovers lay on the pleasantly cold long marble slabs like fingers on a piano keyboard, suspended over the dark valley, the spring and the ruins. It is said that the famous pianist Rubinstein willed his ashes to be dispersed in this forest he loved so much.

## COMPLAINT

The proprietor of a bar in the Russian Compound received complaints from patrons about sounds that filtered into his bar at night and tainted their drinking pleasure. He sent numerous letters to the police, pointing out that these unsettling voices, as he called them, came from the jail across the street, traveling from the interrogation rooms deep under the police station—four, some said six floors underground—all the way up to his bar on the street level. He even visited the police headquarters in person to make his case heard, but the voices persisted. Finally, the bar owner had no choice but to increase the volume of the music playing in his bar during quieter hours. His hearing deteriorated.

## A FUNERAL

ON THE OUTSKIRTS OF TEL-AVIV, IN QIRYAT SHAUL cemetery—named, like most cemeteries in Israel, after suicide king Saul—we watched a small procession slowly making its way down the concrete path, between the stone and concrete gravestones. Most of the mourners were women, who walked and wept in silence. Some men who were present stood back and participated from a distance. We thought: this is the funeral of a woman murdered by a man. The woman actually was, we were soon informed, murdered by her husband. She had written a letter to a popular radio night show host, Halas, addressing him by his first name and begging him for advice on her situation: married to a prominent banker who was rude and sometimes violent, she turned, in her despair, to a man she had been in love with since high school, who agreed to see her, and whom she had begun to meet regularly in secret. She closed her letter by telling the radio host that her life was in danger, beseeching him not to disclose any details about her identity, which would certainly lead to her death. Since Halas had not read the letter before reading it live on the air, this warning had come too late.

# BETWEEN CLASSES

TWO SECOND-YEAR STUDENTS OF HISTORY AT THE Hebrew University could not stand the Faculty of Humanities cafeteria, which they had hated since their very first day in the university. They needed, they agreed, to get away from the octagonal spaces, away from the octagonal tables and the oblique floor that was set to spill them out anyway. They took their lunch next to a secret, narrow, shooting-slit window, the only type of window in the university's fortress-like complex of buildings, between the offices of the department of History and the loftier offices of the department of Philosophy. Sitting on sand-light white-veined marble slab stairs, they leaned their backs on the white walls, looked at the yellow curves of the desert, and chewed on pastrami sandwiches.

## 'AYN LAVAN

ON A SATURDAY MORNING, THE LAVAN FAMILY TOOK us for a walk from their house in Qiryat Menahem, down the mountain slope. We walked past an egg-packing factory, and down toward the valley, on a dusty limestone path. Their eldest, who was my good friend, pointed out a small double-peaked mound of construction refuse, known among neighborhood kids as Ass Mountain. It was early in March, and warm. We followed the vague trail through a wood of pines, crossed two firebreaks, and came upon a pool of water. Tall walnut trees, bare of leaves, their white branches like upraised arms, surrounded the pool. "This is the reservoir, " our friends said, "the spring is up at the end of this open duct. We discovered it, and named it after ourselves, 'Ayn-Lavan, The White Spring." We bathed in the reservoir in our underwear; the water was very cold, and we lay back on the old, gray plastered bank to dry. Later we also took friends to this spring, and told them that we had discovered it, and named it, appropriately, after ourselves.

## THE ROAD TO JERUSALEM

WE MADE THE MOUNTAINS EVERGREEN—LIKE SWITZERland, we liked to say, just like the snowy-peaked mountains in the jigsaw puzzle we liked to assemble with our children — without, naturally, the snow, or the lake (we had to constantly remind ourselves: this is not Switzerland). All along the road to Jerusalem we planted over the past. We covered slopefuls of terraces with pines. The pining hillsides, we dotted with red-tile-roofed houses, but our trees grew sick and stood bare and gray, fell one over the other, dry, and burned for three smoky summer days. An army officer whose regiment happened to have depopulated several villages along what was to become the forested road to Jerusalem, and who later beame a construction contractor in the same region said, in response to the fire, that these trees had done their job, it was now property developers' time.

# SNOW

JUST AS EVERY SUMMER THE DROWNING AT SEA OF inexperienced swimmers from Jerusalem—a city removed from any body of water—is reported with little surprise in the chronicles, so are annual preparations for snow. It falls every second year, between February 15 and March 10, and rarely stays longer than a day. It is celebrated with snowman-building contests, and citizens from the coastal plains are transported to Jerusalem, where they can experience the snow in person. In 1993 however, a snow that had started like any other kept falling for three days with hardly a break. It was reported, as is the habit to report on extreme weather conditions, that even the old men of Safad could not recall such a blizzard. Trees collapsed, blocking roads and knocking down power lines, forcing us to rummage for the old gasoline stove in the basement. We were among the few who defied the orders to stay home. We joined our neighbor for a tour in her car. The city's snowplows could not be brought in from their garage, near Tel-Aviv, and so we had the white roads to ourselves. We found several snowmen and took our pictures next to them, as if we had made them ourselves, to the dismay of the actual snowmen builders. We thought the tour particularly frivolous since, on exiting the neighborhood, the windshield wiper on the driver's side broke down and our neighbor had to rely on verbal instructions. We climbed to the top of a 17-story hotel, but thick clouds and flurries prevented us from getting a good general view of the city, which must be pretty, we thought, under a white blanket. On the fourth day, when the snow began to melt, our other neighbor was found dead in her apartment. It turned out that the old woman, who used to bring us bean soup every Friday, and whom we appreciated deeply for the color and neighborhood feel she gave our street when she sat outside her house on a chair and sorted lentils, had relied on a two-coil electric heater to stay warm.

# FEIGNED

AT THE TEL-AVIV AIRPORT WE MET A MAN WHOM WE had first met in the university, and who lived in the same neighborhood we did, in Jerusalem. This *merry bachelor*, as we came to call him in retrospect, had studied Biology for two years at the Hebrew University, then changed his mind and acquired a B.A. in English Literature, a master's degree in Philosophy, and a master's degree in Psychology, all at the Hebrew University of Jerusalem. He confessed to us, at the airport bar, that he had grown bored of the pick-up scene at the cafeteria, and had therefore left the university. We knew this about him: one woman had him take her to the abortion committee interview, and a week later to the clinic, and home. The woman, daughter of a nurse and a general physician, had been in and out of the psychiatric hospital 'Ezrat Nashim for several years. As a child she used to solicit sick notes from her father to excuse herself from school. Sometimes she feigned illness even to her father. At the age of twelve she pretended to suffer a severe pain in her appendix—having learned that doctors can not rule out a dangerous inflammation, she was taken into hospital, and, too scared to tell the truth, had her appendix removed. From the abortion clinic—only six months after she had cosmetic breast surgery—our neighbor took her to her parents' home. He tucked the comforter around her, left her in her bed, and she never saw him again.

## ONE AFTER THE OTHER

ON HIS DEATHBED, IN JERUSALEM, A SURVIVOR OF seven camps and the death-march of Hungarian Jews confessed to his daughter that he had taken part in the military capture of three villages, and in the deportation of the villagers, and had been a witness to the razing of what houses were left of those villages. His illness had consumed his body to thin fragility. There was time enough for everyone to say good-bye to him and for him to part from them. He made his daughter swear never to tell a soul, and she promised to keep his secret. Driving down the narrow roads off the highway to Tel-Aviv, the daughter looked at the grounds that used to belong to those villages, and hated the forest of pines, funded by our rich supporters in Canada and named, understandably, after them.

# FORGIVEN

In Vienna, a young man from Haifa sat next to us at the hotel breakfast table and burst out with stories about Amsterdam coffee shops and bars, after which he confessed about an episode from his army service. He said he did not regret the damage he had done, and had also been forgiven by the military police. He took the blame onto himself and was released after two days' detention. What he and his friend had done was to sneak out of the barracks, down the mountainside, in the dark. "How can they see you in the night?" he asked his friend, who replied in high short sharp syllables, "Palms are white, palms are white." He used to take the other soldier home with him for weekend leaves, spoil him with his mother's home cooking and take him to Lower-City dance clubs. So thin, so thin and black, the other soldier stood on the lookout, ascertained the car was Arab, and gave the signal to our breakfast companion, who hurled the rock from behind a curve in the road.

## THE NIGHT SKY

THE NIGHT SKY OVER A PICNIC GROUND NEAR KIBBUTZ Qiryat-'Anavim, where our uncle took us, was changed, different from the starlit sky under which he and his comrades had moved in on the site one night, put up fences, built shacks, and took turns patrolling. In his old age, our uncle, whom we loved to visit, collected aerial photographs of the area. With a magnifying glass, and intuition, he pointed out pastures and natural flowerbeds, donkeys, farmer children, olive groves, and even carrots, onions, and lettuces that grew scattered among the olives. So clear was visibility in the years before industrialization, before armored vehicles began grinding the desert sand, that even in winter it was never cloudy for more than a few days in a row. The sky under which a village was bombed out and later razed was not the same sky, over the ground, which was the same, where we had a picnic one dusty day.

# PARTICIPATION

In Tel-Aviv, a random group of Psychology students, who are required to participate in three or four so-called experiments every semester, were asked to imagine the whole city bare, to strip it down in their mind's eye to what it was, or could be. All the students envisioned a big emptiness. They saw streets and buildings, or wide stretches of sand and low bush and a few streams flowing into the sea, some saw ruins. Not one participant in the experiment mentioned humans.

## LISTENER'S REQUEST

OUR FRIEND, WHO LIKED TALK RADIO, WAS TOLD BY the man at the corner falafel stand in Mahne Yuda that he should never have talked the way he did on the call-in show, that he should make religious, and learn what it is to be Jewish. Our friend replied that talking was his way to come close to God, that he had every right to speak out against the militias shooting at peasants and uprooting olive trees in front of the army's open eyes, and that this man's religion was censoring his. Later that afternoon, while making love, our friend asked his wife to replace God's name with his own after the *Oh*.

# COLORS

IN THE LATE 1970S ALL THE KIDS IN THE APARTMENT building where we lived began gathering in our upstairs neighbors' living room to watch television. The Minister of the Treasury had decided to "do good by the people," and had allowed, for the first time, the importation of color televisions. Israeli television, however, was ordered not to broadcast in color, so as not to encourage the poor to spend their savings on expensive imported television sets. Programs and films—most of which were also imported—that were originally produced in color, were consequently filtered through an Eraser that removed the colors, and the signal that went out was black-and-white. One manufacturer was smart enough to produce an Anti-Eraser, which was sold for an additional small fee and restored the colors to the screens. Our neighbors bought an Anti-Eraser, and that's where we'd go to watch cartoons from the US on Saturday morning.

# SUSPECTS

At the beginning of the first Intifada, our reports on the Army Radio news used to announce the deaths of "local inhabitants." When the undercover squads began operating we reported the deaths of "wanted locals." When it became clear that instances of misidentification were occurring quite regularly, we updated the term to "local inhabitants suspected of being wanted." In those days a long series of investigations into bribery by public officials was unfolding, and since none of these officials was even temporarily removed from their position of power, a directive came down from the legal department, instructing us to refer to all suspects under police investigation as "apparent suspects," and to the accusations made against them as "apparent suspicions." Therefore, we also updated our terminology, and began reporting on the deaths of men "suspected of being apparently local."

# TEA OUTDOORS

THE FOURTEEN-YEAR-OLD SENIORS OF THE YOUNG Guardian youth movement learned to taste the land by boiling water in an enamel pot with freshly picked Za'atar stalks and a lot of sugar. Although a stray member may occasionally have taken some home, in general they picked only as many stalks as were necessary for tea, unlike the indigenous peasant women who fill up their bags and sell it on the street. This herb, they learned, is known scientifically as *majoran vulgaris* (in fact, most species of Israeli flora are known scientifically as *vulgaris*, an indication of so much vulgarity not on the part of the plants, but on the part of foreign naturalists who named them), and knowing this they let the teapot boil, and poured into little tin cups. They drank carefully, in little sips, like ghosts that haunt the soil, which is soaked with blood, where vines stretch out over ruins and persist like the claims—big sweet green grapes, rich in seeds, tall fig trees—of the farmers we drove away.

## OBSESSED

A PROFESSOR OF LITERATURE FROM HAIFA, INDEED THE most highly esteemed critic in the country, whose six definitive volumes, *Hebrew Work: Fifty Years of Israeli Prose*, became compulsory reading material for any student of Literature even before they were published, bitterly charged that Hebrew writers are obsessed with death and seem unable to overcome and transcend this obsession. Dead, so dead, the more he told his wife about the goneness of people gone, and insisted that one must leave the past behind, the more his wife resisted. She felt closer to the deceased, who appeared to her to be so fragmented, and yet so whole. "What right have you, who are," she never told him, but he could hear her think, "not just a leech, being a critic, but indeed a maggot, burrowing in dead books, to make such accusations?" The two did not talk frequently.

## PURIM

A WAR WIDOW FROM BAT-YAM MARRIED HER LATE husband's friend, from the same army unit, a young man with whom she then traveled to India. Her new man's commentary on the local service disturbed her so much that a day before reaching the peak on a trek in the Himalayas, she took a solitary lunch break by the creek water, its bed gleaming with the skins of discarded batteries. The tea-shack family's baby approached her, holding a traditional stringed-instrument, and started playing "Yankee Doodle." That day she ran down, in just one day, the distance that had taken them four days to climb. In her room at the lodge in Kathmandu that night, she listened to the radio news in English, which she could not receive up in the mountains, not even on her little short-wave radio, and learned that it was Purim night, and in Hebron a man from Brooklyn had shot dozens of men to death while they were praying in a mosque.

# NEIGHBORS

WE HAD WARNED OUR NEIGHBOR AGAINST BUYING A house in Nahlaot, and indeed he was not welcome there. His new next-door neighbor used to rip his clothes from the shared clothesline stretched across the alley, and drop them onto the limestone pavement. Several times he found trash deposited in the little flowerbed outside his door. Our friend approached his new next-door neighbor, but she, who had lived there for thirty years and did not like newcomers making new rules, did not let him speak. Other neighbors told him they were not on speaking terms with her. His uncle, a therapist who lived on the same alley, told him his neighbor had been very close to the couple from whom he had bought his house, and would not ever forgive them for their break-up and the divorce that ensued. Still, our friend is happy with his little flowerbed, and on his kitchen wall now hangs a large print of his favorite photograph, a close-up of the seam between the neighbor's house and his, her wall covered with rusty tin, and his own newly polished stone wall.

## COMMUNICATION

OUR COUSIN, WHO SOMETIMES TALKS TO HER DEAD sister, and next to whom we sat at Passover dinner, told us she'd had a good meeting with her sister recently, and also felt reassured in her relationship with her boyfriend. It was frequent communication with her sister, she said, that improved her ability to maintain the image of her sister's face longer between the tree tops—the contours against the sky lend themselves to her imagination—when she recalls her. Her sister's openness toward change had helped our cousin forgive her boyfriend's job as a senior engineer at the large rifle-making factory, in Ramat-Hasharon. The boyfriend, who was not invited that evening because of what we considered to be his crassness, later became a sales representative and traveled abroad frequently.

## THE END

SHORTLY AFTER IMMIGRATING, A TRADER FROM WARSAW was given a field in the Yehuda Clan district, as a loan and for safekeeping. He planted an apple orchard and came, in thirty years of apple growing, to appreciate pastoral life so much that he said he'd developed a sense of belonging to the land, which actually meant a sense that the land belonged to him. This farmer then sold what he had come to call his field to a developer because, as he put it, "In the end, all must bend before greed."

# REALIZATION

WE WAITED A LONG TIME AT THE BAR IN THE American Colony Hotel for our friend to join us at the end of his shift. Other patrons did not pay attention to us, but we examined them and immediately recognized the foreign television reporter who hopped around the world from war to war, and whom we could therefore see on our television screens quite often. We quietly traded stories about the heroism of the photographer for an international news agency who was sitting with him, and other such gossip, some of which we made up as we spoke. When a phone call came, at long last, from our friend, who was news editor on the national radio and also read out the hourly news flash five evenings a week, we were disappointed to hear that he would not be joining us in the barely lit room of the bar. He had left work at 11:15PM, we were told, having passed the baton to the night-shift editor, drove his car through Qatamon, a neighborhood removed from anywhere he was supposed to be heading, and continued in the direction of Talpiot, across the Bar'am bridge, where he had an accident. All the while it had not occurred to him that throughout the evening he had been announcing to his listeners that the Bar'am bridge, connecting Qatamon and Talpiot, had collapsed. His colleague, who called us from the hospital to tell us that our friend would not be coming to meet us, described our friend's bafflement at what he now described as his sudden realization that he himself was also implicated by the events on which he reported to the public.

## SYMPTOMS

In a coffee shop in the German Colony neighborhood of Jerusalem we were invited to join the table of our professor and his friend. The professor told us, over a pot of hot chocolate, that symptoms to watch for in trauma survivors are disobedience, hyperactivity, speech difficulties, and aggressive or withdrawn behavior. Exaggerated stories about the traumatic event also occur. Many people you know show at least three of these symptoms, he said, but he had first-hand knowledge of the pathology not only from working with patients, but also from his parents who had fled Europe shortly before the Second World War. Moreover, he said, his son, after his army service, had gone to New York, where he spent some time every day alone on the fire escape outside his window. Roosting on the iron grates, the son reported a rare sense of happiness and a surge of ideas, but when he crossed the window sill to come back in he felt his mouth go dry, very dry. The son wrote down what he saw: always one small pedestrian figure sneaking across the road between cars, trying to catch the drivers' eyes.

ONE WOMAN FROM TEL-AVIV HAD TALKED OPENLY OF her fears for her brother's life when he joined the army. Indeed, he was killed, by so-called friendly fire, after being mistaken for an enemy. She felt immune, as if death had come as close to her as it would for a while. She did not take an interest in the investigation. At twenty, she married a middle-aged media owner who had raped her on the night they met, but whose constant attention and wide knowledge of the world won her heart. None of this, she told us after sharing drugs, was due to the loss of her brother, whose departure, she explained, was final, and well documented, and could therefore arouse no more fear.

# NOSTALGIC

I WAS A NOSTALGIC FROM CHILDHOOD. IN KINDERgarten I longed for my nanny. In first grade I longed for kindergarten. In high school I longed for primary school (which was a horrible experience), and after joining the army I began yearning for kindergarten again, and even, after starting psychoanalysis, discovered a series of very early memories that were, so I learned, significant not in themselves, but in the fact that I had preserved them over so many years, anchors for a deep longing for an early formative age, for the first two years of my life. Having since boarded an airplane and left Israel full of bitter disillusionment and hope for the future, I now long for a time not very long ago, but which I have never known, before ever I existed, or, preferably, before we did.

# STOLEN WATER

LATE ONE SUMMER NIGHT, IN THAT SHORT SEASON after school and before the army, we went for a walk among the old stone villas—typical of Talbiyyeh, the most expensive neighborhood in Jerusalem, where rich Arabs had once lived, the Sa'id family for one, before we threw them out—and saw the rosy clouds of dawn over the trees, between houses that at one time had been more sparse. A yellow truck stopped outside the grocery shop. The driver hauled out two green plastic boxes and left them by the shop door. We helped ourselves to small plastic bags of cold chocolate, and fresh poppy-seed braided rolls. We had to sneak into several yards and check stairways to find a copy of *Haaretz*. It announced, in the cold-blooded tone of diplomats and foreign journalists, that in the coastal plain a civilian bus had been hijacked late that night. We punned: a stolen newspaper carries stronger news, the way that *stolen water is sweeter*. Earlier that year, on the Day of Memory, the principle had convened us—all wearing the national colors: white shirts and blue pants—and read out the names of all the school graduates who had died in wars. "Every year," he said, "we tell you of our hope that you, the younger ones, will not *have to* serve in the army, will not go to war. But, I am sorry to say, that day has not yet arrived." The custom in those days was to withhold the names of the dead from the public until seven in the morning, allowing a pause to inform relatives during the night. We listened to the morning news and our breathing eased when no one we knew was among the seventeen names the announcer read, reliable, serious, and resolved.

# TWO POINTS

A FOREST FIRE HAD FORCED OUR DRIVER, IN A SERVICE taxi from Tel-Aviv to Jerusalem, to divert from the highway, onto a narrow backroad. The scenic route we found ourselves on, a little Garden of Eden, as one of the passengers called it, generated an unexpected quiet intimacy among the seven passengers and the driver, spoiled only by the crackling voice of a man who was annoyed by the view. What began as a murmur from this man, who sat next to the driver and was a cartographer for the Measuring Center, soon turned into a lecture, to which we all had to listen. At no *single point*, this man said, were all the names removed from the old map and the new map, with new Zionist names, was drawn. He directed our gaze across the forested slopes, up to some red-tile-roofed houses strewn about the mountain top. The village of Bayt Thul, for example, he said, was only renamed Nataf in 1982, when its land and ruins were auctioned off by the state. The cartographer was a broad-faced man who had graduated in draughtsmanship from the Academy of Art in Warsaw, he said, and had acquired a professional certificate in London. From time to time he wiped the sweat off his forehead with a white handkerchief from the pocket of his jacket. He never removed his jacket, even though the day was hot. The *turning point* was, he went on, not bothering to inquire if anyone was interested in what he had to say, in the late 1940s, when the decision to leave only a few villages intact was taken and carried out, although the exact number of villages and townships depopulated that year still arouses scholarly debate. Suddenly, another village caught his eye. This locality, he said, is still known as Abu Ghosh.

## SECRETS

A MAN IN QIRYAT ONO DIED OF A STROKE BEFORE HIS grandson was old enough to see his Red Army insignia, acquired in exchange for milk at a displaced people's camp in northern Bavaria. No witness survived to tell the man's family of his real work during World War II.

# A LETTER

In the Cafe De La Presse, in Paris, we met a colleague who had disappeared several years earlier, shortly after he was appointed editor-in-chief of a prestigious magazine. We had ordered two *petits cremes*, and to our surprise it was not the waiter who emerged from the kitchen and delivered the coffee to our table, but our colleague, dressed as a kitchen worker. He told us that on his first day on the new job at the magazine he had lost not only his professional confidence but also his personal sense of direction. For the first time in his career of nineteen years he had been given his own office, and a secretary to screen his calls. Sitting at his new desk, he said, looking through his window at the rows of cubicles in front of him (cheap board boxes and run-down chairs with which he was only too familiar), he could not recall any of his ideas for beautiful things the magazine could do for its readers and for the city—dreams he had nurtured for years (first as a young contributor to the consumer section, then as an adult freelance writer, staff writer, and later as section editor and deputy editor), nor the reason he had become a journalist in the first place. By the end of his first day in the new position he felt himself sinking fast into melancholy. His job, he suddenly realized, was to serve not the readers but big advertisers, first and foremost real estate developers, who provided the bulk of the magazine's income. His salary—a sum that for the first time in his life could allow him a modest luxury—seemed to be nothing but a bribe. He composed his letter of resignation that night, as well as a letter to the readers, explaining his despair. He announced to the readers his decision to leave the country in search of refuge, and promised to send a card from his new homeland, once he was settled. This was but a passing phase, our colleague said, and fortunately it was recognized as such by his replacement, who in consultation with the editor in charge of the Letters section, chose not to print his letter.

# SUSPICIOUS OBJECT

In the St. Louis airport smoking lounge, a stinking glass aquarium with seats in a circle, we met our childhood neighbor, who still kept his parents' old apartment in the building we had all once lived in, and used it as an office. The hills around there, he told us, are now buried under the red-tile-roofed stone houses of a new neighborhood, or a development—there is no difference by now—and named after the developer. We were greatly saddened to learn that not a piece of soil was exposed of the wild hills where we once went with our neighbor on a suspicious objects hunt, when we were all still in primary school. Impressed by public service announcements on television and posters that we studied in school corridors, we were familiar with every black-and-white image of common handmade so-called bombs. The posters read: Don't Touch A Suspicious Object, Lest You Get Hurt. When on our hunt we came upon a metal cylinder, we easily identified it as a Button Mine, and knew what to do. We enclosed the object with a circle of rocks (to ward off the innocent) and reported our findings to the police. The policemen were indignant to find a rusty kettle-top, with a black plastic holder in the middle, twenty paces from the road in the brush.

## SURPRISE

In the Yizr'ael valley, formerly known as Marj Ibn-'Amer, where the inhabitants of almost two-thirds of the indigenous villages were allowed to keep their houses, though not their land, our friend, whose family was also allowed to stay in their house, told us how, as a youth, he used to go out and search for the sandal Jesus is said to have dropped in mid-leap from Nazareth to Mount Tabor. Our friend then took us to the nearby Museum of Bedouin Heritage, where a black goat-hair tent, a wooden plow, and various artifacts dating from the 1960s and 1970s are exhibited to illustrate for us, we surmised, how our ancient shepherd ancestors had lived. We thought it strange that there was no camel in the exhibit. Our friend was surprised to discover his old classmate from the regional high school seated inside the tent, pounding coffee beans with a traditional pestle and mortar. "What are you doing here," he asked, and his friend replied, "I am the Sheikh on duty."

## A SHORT STORY

A PROFESSOR OF FRENCH AT THE HEBREW UNIVERSITY fascinated students with subversive literary criticism and radical interpretations of history. During a class trip—naturally, to France—students were kept well informed of the affair the professor was having with one of them. They knew that professor and student were secretly sharing his room, that his wife didn't know, that neither did her husband. The details were discussed openly, but not in the professor's presence. About their fights: "Don't be surprised if he's nervous today," the student lover announced one morning at the breakfast table. "Couldn't get it up last night." Some students were envious: fifty, brilliant, humorous and in shape, everything one could expect in a man of this genre. Some wondered if it was possible for this to grow even more embarrassingly intimate. It ended when the class returned to Jerusalem. Word had reached his wife. "There are no *romans*," he said when the class next convened. He paused for effect, and brushed a black forelock with his long fingers, "Long orderly texts belong in the 19th-century shelves. Today, there are only short stories."

# ACQUISITION

SELF-CONGRATULATORY CONVERSATION IS PART OF Israeli decorum, and confirming that *our beauty is in our problemacy* is common about the dinner table. "How beautiful a language is ours," said a linguist to his companion in an Arab restaurant. "How open and accomodating it is" (read: we are so open and accomodating). "We say this coffee is *ya'ani 'ala kefak. 'Ala kefak,* superb; *ya'ani,* that is to say. Arabic words, adopted by our ever-absorbent language. But the Hebrew *'ala kefak* is not identical to the Arab. When, for example, I order Turkish coffee, and loudly insist on having it cooked in a particular way, with the spice added in the grinding, the Arab waiter shows me his palms in desperation and mutters *'Ala kefak,* as you please." (See illustration: Six militia members are sitting around a camp fire out in a field. From the right: Yosske, 23, already big-bellied, repeats his urban rabbit-hunting joke. Bracha, 25, in khakis like all of them and a brown sweater, is holding a little cup out to Kish, 28, with the handlebar moustache. Shmil, crouching, starts singing a camp-fire waltz. Shuki, 31, is the only one in the picture wearing the typical woolen *sock hat*, which is otherwise known as a ski mask—it does get cold, and for some actions they like to cover their faces. Everyone joins in the long series of hearty Russian diphthongs *Lay, la la lay* building up for the thirsty *Round and round goes the finjan*, repeated four times. *Finjan*, meaning the pot. Their clothes are soaked with smoke. In the Arabic, however, *finjan* denotes a cup.) Of course, many words remain, unadopted, with the people of this country, *ya'ani Falastin*. Try saying it.

# THE GOOD GUIDE

THE NEW TOURIST GUIDE, WHO KNOWS EVEN LESS about the history of the country than the old tourist guide, supplies better service by following the Friendly Guide Regulations issued by the Ministry of Tourism and leading visitors along the newly marked Friendly Path through the city. He doesn't touch on what we all know. He spices his speech with the occasional Hebrew and Arabic, tints his talk with happy anecdotes and references. Thus he cheers tourists as they descend upon more and more servants, cleaners, waiters, sex workers, and bell-boys, who are all better trained than ever.

# HABIT

ON A CLASS TRIP IN THE JUDEAN DESERT, A TEACHER fell off a mountain cliff, after which a rule was established in our school: trips to flat areas only. We were glad, therefore, when our mother took us away to the Pyrenees for the *Sukkot* break, where we travelled in a rented car. Out of habit we switched on the radio on the hour, in a forest in Catalonia, and scanned the airwaves for the news. We heard the inflected name of our city on the news, "Jerusalema," twice. On the next hour we stopped by the side of the road and sat prepared to listen. We could make out the words "dos bombas." That night we took a room with global television and saw pictures from the produce market very near our home. Our mother telephoned the neighbors and her good friend, since the bombs exploded on the day of the week and around the time that she and her friend usually go shopping in the market. Once it was ascertained that no one close to us was hurt, we took turns in the bathtub. Our habit hardened.

**Oz Shelach** was born in West Jerusalem in 1968 and has been a journalist and editor for Israeli radio and magazines. He currently lives in New York and runs a small news service and art gallery, oznik.com.